PEACHTREE

Loose Tooth

A Viking Easy-to-Read

Story by **Anastasia Suen**
Illustrations by **Allan Eitzen**

Based on the characters created by
Ezra Jack Keats

VIKING

VIKING
Published by the Penguin Group
Penguin Putnam Books for Young Readers,
345 Hudson Street, New York, New York 10014, U.S.A.
Penguin Books Ltd, 27 Wrights Lane, London W8 5TZ, England
Penguin Books Australia Ltd, Ringwood, Victoria, Australia
Penguin Books Canada Ltd, 10 Alcorn Avenue, Toronto, Ontario, Canada M4V 3B2
Penguin Books (N.Z.) Ltd, 182-190 Wairau Road, Auckland 10, New Zealand

Penguin Books Ltd, Registered Offices: Harmondsworth, Middlesex, England

First published in 2002 by Viking,
a division of Penguin Putnam Books for Young Readers.

1 3 5 7 9 10 8 6 4 2

Text by Anastasia Suen
Illustrations by Allan Eitzen

LIBRARY OF CONGRESS CATALOGING-IN-PUBLICATION DATA
Suen, Anastasia.
Loose tooth / by Anastasia Suen ; illustrated by Allan Eitzen;
based on characters created by Ezra Jack Keats.
p. cm.
Summary: Peter can't decide if he wants his loose tooth to fall out because
if it falls out, he will have a gap in his smile for the school pictures,
but money from the tooth fairy will help him buy a new basketball.
ISBN 0-670-03536-X (hardcover)
[1. Teeth—Fiction. 2. Basketball—Fiction. 3. African Americans—Fiction.]
I. Eitzen, Allan, ill. II. Keats, Ezra Jack. III. Title.
PZ7.S94343 Lo 2002
[E]—dc21
2001002873

Viking® and Easy-to-Read® are registered trademarks of Penguin Putnam Inc.

Printed in Hong Kong
Set in Bookman

Reading Level: 1.8

Loose Tooth

It was picture day, and Peter's tooth was loose.

He wiggled it with his tongue at the bus stop.

"Are you okay?" asked Archie. "You look funny."

"My tooth is loose," said Peter.

"I thought you lost your front teeth already," said Amy.

"I did," said Peter. "But now this other one is loose."

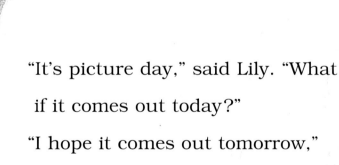

"It's picture day," said Lily. "What
if it comes out today?"
"I hope it comes out tomorrow,"
said Peter.
"I want one school picture without
a hole in my smile. Last year my
two front teeth were out."

Roar! Squeak!

"Here's the bus," said Amy.

Peter, Archie, Lily, and Amy climbed on the bus.

"What about the tooth fairy?" asked Lily.

"If you lose your tooth, you could use
the money from the tooth fairy."

"You have been saving for that basketball,"
said Archie.

"I saw it in the store window," said Amy.

Peter sighed.

"I really want that basketball," he said.

"But I don't want a hole in my smile
on picture day."

"Say cheese," said Lily.

Peter smiled.

"So far, so good," said Archie.

"There's no hole."

"You can't even tell it's loose," said Amy.

"Just don't wiggle it," said Lily.

"That's an idea," said Peter. "I won't wiggle it."

The bus stopped at school.

"An open court," yelled Archie. "I'll save it for us."

They ran off the bus.

"I'll get the ball," said Peter.

He ran over to the ball bin.

There was one basketball left.

One of the boys in Room 3 grabbed the ball first.

"Hey!" said Peter.

"It's my ball," said the boy.

"We were here first," said a tall girl from Room 3.

Two more kids from Room 3 came over.

Peter looked at the kids from Room 3.

"We have the court, and you have the ball,"

he said. "Let's play."

"We play to win," said the boy.

"So do we," said Peter.

The boy from Room 3 threw the ball in.

The tall girl dribbled it.

She passed it to another kid from Room 3.

He jumped, and he scored!

"Hey!" said Lily. "I thought this was our game."

"It is," said Peter. "Just watch."

Peter threw the ball to Archie.

Archie dribbled and passed to Amy.

Peter ran under the basket.

The boy from Room 3 elbowed

his way in front of Peter.

Peter stepped around him.

Archie tossed the ball to Peter
and Peter jumped.
The ball went in. Two points!

The boy frowned.

"We're going to win," said the boy.

"You haven't won yet," said Peter.

The kids from Room 3

scored two baskets in a row.

"We're losing!" said Lily.

"No, we're just warming up," said Amy,

and she passed the ball to Archie.

Archie looked at Peter.

Peter ran under the basket.

The same boy stepped in front of Peter.

He moved his arms back and forth.

Archie tossed the ball to Peter.

The boy batted it away.

Lily scrambled and grabbed the ball.

She passed the ball to Peter.

Peter jumped and shot the ball.

The boy bumped into Peter.

Bam! Peter hit the ground.

Slam! The ball hit the backboard

and dropped through the net.

Ring! The school bell rang.

The kids in Room 3 ran off to class.

Archie helped Peter off the ground.

"Are you okay?" asked Lily.

"We almost beat them," said Amy.

Peter put his hand to his mouth.

He leaned over.

The tooth fell out into his hand.

"Uh-oh," said Archie.

"Oh, Peter," said Lily.

"What are you going to do?" asked Amy.

Peter smiled.

"I'm going to buy a basketball," he said.

"Say cheese!"